A Note to Parents

Welcome to REAL KIDS READERS, a series of phonics-based books for children who are beginning to read. In the classroom, educators use phonics to teach children how to sound out unfamiliar words, providing a firm foundation for reading skills. At home, you can use REAL KIDS READERS to reinforce and build on that foundation, because the books follow the same basic phonic guidelines that children learn in school.

Of course the best way to help your child become a good reader is to make the experience fun—and REAL KIDS READERS do that, too. With their realistic story lines and lively characters, the books engage children's imaginations. With their clean design and sparkling photographs, they provide picture clues that help new readers decipher the text. The combination is sure to entertain young children and make them truly want to read.

REAL KIDS READERS have been developed at three distinct levels to make it easy for children to read at their own pace.

- LEVEL 1 is for children who are just beginning to read.
- LEVEL 2 is for children who can read with help.
- LEVEL 3 is for children who can read on their own.

A controlled vocabulary provides the framework at each level. Repetition, rhyme, and humor help increase word skills. Because children can understand the words and follow the stories, they quickly develop confidence. They go back to each book again and again, increasing their proficiency and sense of accomplishment, until they're ready to move on to the next level. The result is a rich and rewarding experience that will help them develop a lifelong love of reading.

For Dad and Tessa—
you know this story already
—L. P.

For my mother, Sally, a true original,
with love
—D. H.

Special thanks to Lands' End, Dodgeville, WI,
for providing Ted and Tony's clothing.

Produced by DWAI / Seventeenth Street Productions, Inc.
Reading Specialist: Virginia Grant Clammer

Library of Congress Cataloging-in-Publication Data
Papademetriou, Lisa.
  Lucky me! / Lisa Papademetriou ; photographs by Dorothy Handelman.
      p.   cm. — (Real kids readers. Level 3)
  Summary: Ted is embarrassed by his unusual grandmother but when she takes him to
a ballgame and helps him catch a home run ball, he decides she's pretty cool after all.
  ISBN 0-7613-2071-1 (lib. bdg.). — ISBN 0-7613-2096-7 (pbk.)
  [1. Grandmothers—Fiction. 2. Baseball—Fiction.] I. Handelman, Dorothy, ill. II. Title.
III. Series.
PZ7.P1954Lu   1999
[E]—dc21   98-52505
                                                                        CIP
                                                                        AC

pbk: 10 9 8 7 6 5 4 3 2 1
lib: 10 9 8 7 6 5 4 3 2 1

Lucky Me!

By Lisa Papademetriou
Photographs by Dorothy Handelman

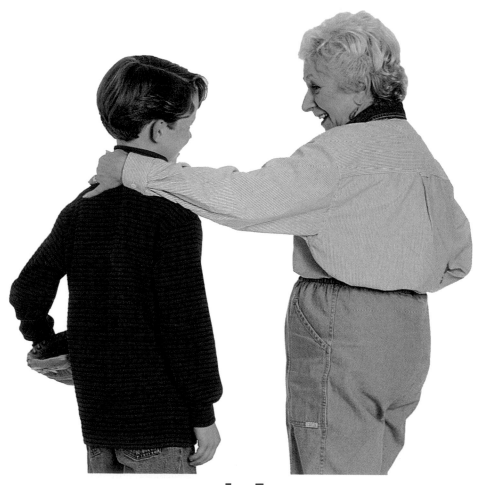

![M]

The Millbrook Press
Brookfield, Connecticut

Don't get me wrong. I love my grandma. But I have to say she doesn't act like other grandmas at all!

Other grandmas wear dresses. My grandma wears jeans. Other grandmas like to play cards. My grandma likes to play baseball and soccer and touch football. Other grandmas bake pies and cookies. My grandma makes salads with bean sprouts.

My grandma lives with me and my parents, and sometimes she drives me crazy. For example, my name is Ted. But Grandma calls me Teddy Bear—in front of my friends! Also, she has a very loud laugh. Believe me. When she laughs, everyone turns to look. And if I ask her to shush, she says, "What's wrong, Teddy Bear?" in a very loud voice. It's totally embarrassing.

I think it would be nice to have a grandma who sits in a rocking chair and knits. That's what I think the perfect grandma would do.

I talked to my friend Tony about it when he came over one Friday after school.

"You're lucky," I said. "Your grandma knits sweaters for you. She bakes you good things to eat. She never embarrasses you."

"No, you're lucky," he said. "The sweaters my grandma knits are hot and scratchy. Besides, she doesn't play catch like your grandma does, and she doesn't tell jokes either."

There was a knock on my bedroom door. "Knock, knock," said Grandma.

I groaned, but Tony played along. "Who's there?" he asked.

"Wanda," said Grandma.

"Wanda who?" asked Tony.

"Wanda go play catch?" asked Grandma.

Tony laughed. He opened the door, and Grandma came in.

"Last one to the backyard is an old potato!" she cried. Then she raced off.

"See how lucky you are?" Tony and I said together. Then we both laughed.

"Actually, I have to go," said Tony. "It's almost dinnertime."

I grabbed my baseball glove and walked Tony to the door. Then I went around to the backyard.

"I guess it's just you and me, Teddy Bear," said Grandma. "Try to catch this one." She threw the ball high in the air.

13

You wouldn't believe how far my grandma can throw! I ran all the way back to the fence. I jumped high. *Thud!* I caught the ball right in the center of my glove.

"Great catch!" called Grandma. "Pretty soon you'll be as good as the Rocket."

"Thanks, Grandma," I said.

Mike "the Rocket" Stone plays right field for the Jets, my city's baseball team. Grandma and I are his biggest fans. He can catch any ball hit into right field. And when he hits the ball, it's like a rocket heading for the moon.

I want to be just like him.

After a while, my dad called us to come in for dinner.

"Hey," Grandma said as we headed inside. "How would you like to go to the ball game tomorrow? It's the first one of the season."

"I'd love to!" I told her. "Only, you won't call me Teddy Bear at the ballpark, will you?"

Grandma just laughed her loud laugh.

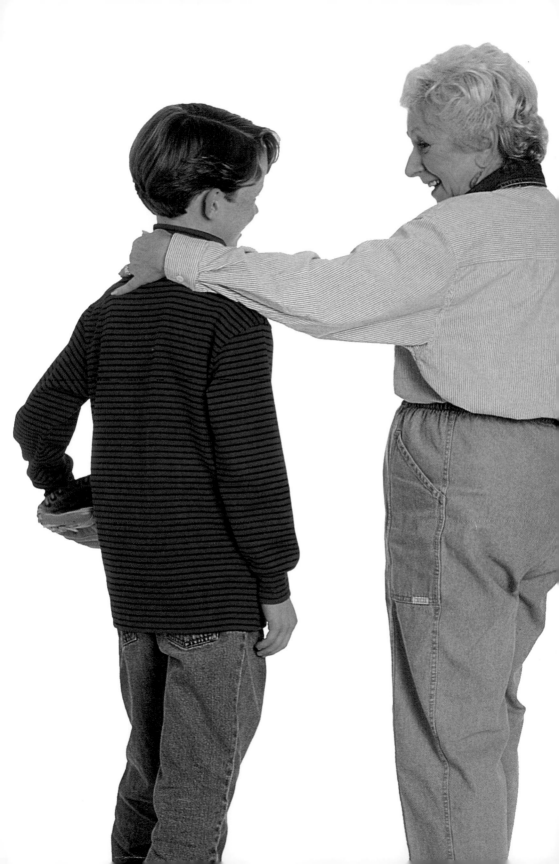

The game was Saturday afternoon. When it was time to go, I grabbed my baseball glove. I wanted to be ready in case someone hit a ball into the stands near me. I dashed downstairs—and stopped short. "Grandma!" I said. "Is that what you're wearing to the ballpark?"

"Yes," said Grandma. "Isn't it great?"
I bit my lip. I was glad I had a grandma who wanted to take me to the ball game. But did she have to act so nutty?

On the way to the ballpark, Grandma played loud rock and roll on the car radio. She sang along. Lucky for me, the windows were up, so nobody could hear.

Grandma parked the car, and we walked to the ticket line.

For a while she behaved. She stood in line quietly. She didn't call me Teddy Bear. She didn't laugh her loud laugh. But the line was long, and soon she began to get restless.

"I don't want you to miss the first pitch," she told me. "Besides, I shouldn't have to wait in line. I am a grandmother!"

She grabbed my arm and pulled me around to the front of the line.

"Excuse me, sir," she said to the man standing there. "May we go next? I don't want my grandson to miss the first pitch. This is his first baseball game."

I couldn't believe my ears. "Grandma!" I said. "I've been to lots of games!"

"I know," she whispered back. "But it's your first game this year, isn't it?"

The man gave me a wink. "Go right ahead," he said, waving us on.

"Thank you," said Grandma.

Then she noticed that the man was smoking a cigar. "Excuse me," she said again. "That cigar is very smelly. Would you please put it out? I'm worried that it will bother my grandson."

The man looked at me, and I felt my face get hot.

"See?" Grandma said. "He's turning red already. It's probably because of the smoke."

The man put out his cigar and grinned at me. "Don't be embarrassed. Everyone has a grandmother," he said.

"Not like mine," I said.

Our seats were behind right field. We found them just in time to sing the national anthem. Grandma sang loudly, of course, but this time I didn't mind. Everyone was singing that way.

The top half of the first inning was short. The first two batters struck out. The third hit a fly ball that was caught in center field.

It was the Jets' turn to bat!

Just then the hot-dog man walked by.

"Hot dogs!" he called. "Get your red-hot hot dogs."

"Over here!" Grandma called. "My grandson wants one."

"Grandma!" I said.

"What is it, Teddy Bear?" she asked loudly.

I sank in my seat.

The hot-dog man came over.

"My grandson would like a nice big hot dog," Grandma said. "He's very hungry."

The hot-dog man looked over his tray of hot dogs. "This is the best of the bunch," he said, holding one out.

"Good," she said. "Now will you add some mustard, ketchup, and pickle relish?" She smiled sweetly. "My grandson loves pickle relish."

The hot-dog man looked at me. "Does he?"

I smiled weakly and nodded.

He fixed the hot dog. But when he tried to give it to me, Grandma took it.

"I'll just check to make sure it's okay," she said. She studied the hot dog carefully. She gave it a sniff. Then she handed it over.

Grandma was driving me crazy! But when I took a bite of the hot dog, I had to admit it was perfect. "Thanks, Grandma," I said.

Ten minutes later, the Rocket stepped up to the plate, and Grandma went wild! She jumped up and down. She waved her pom-poms. She shouted out a cheer.

"Rocket, Rocket, hit that ball!
Knock it, Rocket, to the wall!"

I tried to hide in the hood of my sweatshirt. If someone from school saw me with my crazy grandmother, my life would be over! Luckily, the Rocket hit a double, and Grandma sat down.

"See?" she said. "Cheering helps."

After that, Grandma performed her cheer every time the Rocket was at bat. She held up her sign every time he headed out to right field.

During the seventh-inning stretch, Grandma got to her feet. "All right, Ted. Let's go!" she cried. "We're going to do fifty jumping jacks."

"Grandma! People will stare," I said.

"Let them," she said. "We've been sitting too long."

She pulled me away from the seats and began jumping up and down. I tried to do the smallest jumping jacks I could. Even so, I was sure everyone noticed.

Finally we finished and sat back down.

In the bottom of the next inning, the Rocket came up to bat. The bases were loaded, so Grandma started a new cheer.

"Rocket! Rocket! He's our man.
He's going to hit a great big slam."

Then the Rocket did something I'd never seen him do before. He pointed his bat at the right-field stands.

"See that?" Grandma demanded. "The Rocket is pointing straight at us! He likes my cheer."

I rolled my eyes. The Rocket wasn't really pointing at us. Or was he?

The Rocket swung at the first pitch.
Crack! He hit the ball hard. It looked
like a home run—and it was headed our
way. Could I reach it?

"Go for it, Ted!" Grandma yelled, and
she lifted me onto the seat.

I stretched up . . . up. . . . *Thud!* The ball hit my glove.

"You did it!" Grandma cried.

I couldn't believe it. I'd caught the Rocket's home-run ball! But I never could have done it without Grandma's help.

"You should have this," I told her, holding out the ball. "It was your cheer that made the ball come this way. Besides, the Rocket is your hero."

Grandma shook her head. "The Rocket is my other hero," she told me. "You're the biggest hero in my book."

"Thanks, Grandma," I said. "I'll keep this forever."

The Jets won, thanks to the Rocket's big hit. Guess who got him to sign the home-run ball after the game?

When we got to the car, Grandma cranked up the radio and sang along— as usual.

I looked down at my baseball, and suddenly I realized something. Tony was right. I was lucky to have such a cool grandma.

We sang all the way home.

Reading with Your Child

Even though your child is reading more independently now, it is vital that you continue to take part in this important learning experience.

- Try to read with your child at least twenty minutes each day, as part of your regular routine.
- Encourage your child to keep favorite books in one convenient, cozy spot, so you don't waste valuable reading time looking for them.
- Read and familiarize yourself with the Phonic Guidelines on the next pages.
- Praise your young reader. Be the cheerleader, not the teacher. Your enthusiasm and encouragement are key ingredients in your child's success.

What to Do if Your Child Gets Stuck on a Word

- Wait a moment to see if he or she works it out alone.
- Help him or her decode the word phonetically. Say, "Try to sound it out."
- Encourage him or her to use picture clues. Say, "What does the picture show?"
- Encourage him or her to use context clues. Say, "What would make sense?"
- Ask him or her to try again. Say, "Read the sentence again and start the tricky word. Get your mouth ready to say it."
- If your child still doesn't "get" the word, tell him or her what it is. Don't wait for frustration to build.

What to Do if Your Child Makes a Mistake

- If the mistake makes sense, ignore it—unless it is part of a pattern of errors you wish to correct.
- If the mistake doesn't make sense, wait a moment to see if your child corrects it.
- If your child doesn't correct the mistake, ask him or her to try again, either by decoding the word or by using context or picture clues. Say, "Get your mouth ready" or "Make it sound right" or "Make it make sense."
- If your child still doesn't "get" the word, tell him or her what it is. Don't wait for frustration to build.

Phonic Guidelines

Use the following guidelines to help your child read the words in this story.

Short Vowels

When two consonants surround a vowel, the sound of the vowel is usually short. This means you pronounce *a* as in apple, *e* as in egg, *i* as in igloo, *o* as in octopus, and *u* as in umbrella. Words with short vowels include: *bed, big, box, cat, cup, dad, dog, get, hid, hop, hum, jam, kid, mad, met, mom, pen, ran, sad, sit, sun, top.*

R-Controlled Vowels

When a vowel is followed by the letter *r*, its sound is changed by the *r*. Words with *r*-controlled vowels include: *card, curl, dirt, farm, girl, herd, horn, jerk, torn, turn.*

Long Vowel and Silent E

If a word has a vowel followed by a consonant and an *e*, usually the vowel is long and the *e* is silent. Long vowels are pronounced the same way as their alphabet names. Words with a long vowel and silent *e* include: *bake, cute, dive, game, home, kite, mule, page, pole, ride, vote.*

Double Vowels

When two vowels are side by side, usually the first vowel is long and the second vowel is silent. Words with double vowels include: *boat, clean, gray, loaf, meet, neat, paint, pie, play, rain, sleep, tried.*

Diphthongs

Sometimes when two vowels (or a vowel and a consonant) are side by side, they combine to make a diphthong—a sound that is different from long or short vowel sounds. Diphthongs are: *au/aw, ew, oi/oy, ou/ow.* Words with diphthongs include: *auto, brown, claw, flew, found, join, toy.*

Double Consonants

When two identical consonants appear side by side, one of them is silent. Words with double consonants include: *bell, fuss, mess, mitt, puff, tall, yell.*

Consonant Blends

When two or more different consonants are side by side, they usually blend to make a combined sound. Words with consonant blends include: *bent, blob, bride, club, crib, drop, flip, frog, gift, glare, grip, help, jump, mask, most, pink, plane, ring, send, skate, sled, spin, steep, swim, trap, twin.*

Consonant Digraphs

Sometimes when two different consonants are side by side, they make a digraph that represents a single new sound. Consonant digraphs are: *ch, sh, th, wh*. Words with digraphs include: *bath, chest, lunch, sheet, think, whip, wish*.

Silent Consonants

Sometimes, when two different consonants are side by side, one of them is silent. Words with silent consonants include: *back, dumb, knit, knot, lamb, sock, walk, wrap, wreck*.

Sight Words

Sight words are those words that a reader must learn to recognize immediately—by sight—instead of by sounding them out. They occur with high frequency in easy texts. Sight words include: *a, am, an, and, as, at, be, big, but, can, come, do, for, get, give, have, he, her, his, I, in, is, it, just, like, look, make, my, new, no, not, now, old, one, out, play, put, red, run, said, see, she, so, some, soon, that, the, then, there, they, to, too, two, under, up, us, very, want, was, we, went, what, when, where, with, you*.

Exceptions to the "Rules"

Although much of the English language is phonically regular, there are many words that don't follow the above guidelines. For example, a particular combination of letters can represent more than one sound. Double *oo* can represent a long *oo* sound, as in words such as *boot, cool,* and *moon;* or it can represent a short *oo* sound, as in words such as *foot, good,* and *hook*. The letters *ow* can represent a diphthong, as in words such as *brow, fowl,* and *town;* or they can represent a long *o* sound, as in words such as *blow, snow,* and *tow*. Additionally, some high-frequency words such as *some, come, have,* and *said* do not follow the guidelines at all, and *ough* appears in such different-sounding words as *although, enough,* and *thought*.

The phonic guidelines provided in this book are just that—guidelines. They do not cover all the irregularities in our rich and varied language, but are intended to correspond roughly to the phonic lessons taught in the first and second grades. Phonics provides the foundation for learning to read. Repetition, visual clues, context, and sheer experience provide the rest.